# Lizzie's List

By the same author
*Angels on Roller Skates*

# Lizzie's List

## Maggie Harrison
illustrated by Bethan Matthews

CANDLEWICK PRESS
CAMBRIDGE, MASSACHUSETTS

Text copyright © 1991 by Maggie Harrison
Illustrations copyright © 1991 by Bethan Matthews

First U.S. edition 1993
First published in Great Britain in 1991 by Walker Books Ltd., London.

Library of Congress Cataloging-in-Publication Data

Harrison, Maggie.
Lizzie's list / Maggie Harrison; illustrated by Bethan Matthews.—
1st U.S. ed.
First published in Great Britain in 1991 by Walker Books Ltd., London.
Summary: Lizzie lives alone with her mother, but she wishes she
had other relatives, so she 'adopts' a grandmother and others to make
her own large family.
ISBN 1-56402-197-1
[1. Family life—Fiction.   2. Single-parent family—Fiction.   3.
Grandmothers—Fiction.]   I. Matthews, Bethan, ill.   II. Title.
PZ7.H253Li   1993   92-54580
[Fic]—dc20

10 9 8 7 6 5 4 3 2 1

Printed in the United States

The pictures in this book were done in pen and ink.

Candlewick Press
2067 Massachusetts Avenue
Cambridge, Massachusetts 02140

To adoptions in general
and to Tabitha, Charity,
and John in particular,
because they will know why.

# Contents

# First Catch Your Grandma

Lizzie was a girl who usually got what she wanted. And not by whining, screaming, or throwing a tantrum. Maybe she was just more realistic than most nine-year-olds. After all, if you cry for the moon you are usually left moonless and still crying. When Lizzie wanted something, she *made* it happen, instead of hanging around hoping that somebody else would do it for her. And that's why all this began.

One Saturday afternoon she came into the kitchen and said, "Mom, where's my grand-mother?"

Her mother looked surprised, but went on ironing.

"She died, Lizzie, you know she did. When

you were only ten months old. We've been through all this before. It was sad, but she was old and very sick."

"Well, what about my other one, then? Lucy has two grandmothers."

"You mean your dad's mother? She died too, even longer ago. I never even knew her."

"So there are no grandmas. And no grandpas left, either?"

"Sorry, honey. It's a shame, because it's nice

to have grandparents."

"Lucy goes to stay with hers and they spoil her. She likes it. They have a house near the sea, one set of them does, and *her* grandma . . ."

"Well, I'm sorry we didn't manage things better for you, Lizzie, but nobody lasts forever, and there's nothing we can do about it. Your friend Lucy talks too much!"

Mom smoothed the cotton slacks on the ironing board; then she smiled.

"I'm sorry there aren't any grandmother stores, or I'd save up and buy one for you!"

"Don't be silly, Mom," Lizzie said, and wandered away. She trailed down seven flights of concrete stairs, thinking, and crossed over to the grassy play area between the tall blocks of apartments. She sat on a swing, still thinking, and rubbed a deep groove in the hard-packed earth with the edge of her sneakers. Then she trailed all the way back to the apartment.

"And there aren't any uncles or aunts, are there? Or cousins or anything? Just me and you."

"That's right, Lizzie, just you and me."

Lizzie went to her room, closed the door, found a felt-tip pen that still worked, and made a list.

"That's what I need," she said to herself. Then Mom called her for supper and they watched some skating on TV.

The following Saturday Lizzie wandered around the shopping district watching all the elderly ladies. She had decided to find a grandma for herself, but she wasn't at all sure how to choose one. She wished that she could have seen Lucy's grandmothers first, to give her some idea of what to look for.

There were a lot of older women shopping that morning, but none of them seemed quite right. Lizzie sighed. It was more difficult than she'd expected. The ones with well-cut hair, bounding along with loud hearty laughs and expensive, sensible shoes, looked like hard work. But the ones who pushed shopping carts, stopping to blink at all the crowds, weren't quite right either.

Lizzie sat down on a concrete bench, feeling

discouraged. She had to admit that she knew absolutely nothing about real grandmothers, or even what made a good one. Why hadn't she asked Mom what her own grandma had been like? Rather dark photographs in an old album showed her holding Lizzie as a baby. Now Lizzie felt a little ashamed to remember that she had always been more interested in looking at the baby than at the person holding her. She wasn't even sure what she wanted a grandmother to do. Other than belong to her, of course. And to stop her from being so jealous of Lucy. Somebody she could visit, maybe, and who could come to school with her mom to see the end-of-year play or to sports day. Maybe she should ask Lucy to bring some photographs to school . . .

Lizzie was so busy trying to imagine what Lucy's grandmothers looked like, that she hardly noticed the elderly woman walking toward her bench. But when the woman sat down, Lizzie glanced at her automatically. This one was definitely too severe. More like a retired schoolteacher than a grandma, with that narrow, bony head and those sharp eyes. And she was scruffy. The corners of her coat pockets needed sewing up. Proper grandmothers always mended clothes and said things like "a stitch in time saves nine." And she wasn't sure grandmothers were supposed to wear dark red corduroy pants, like this one had on. It didn't seem suitable somehow. And her hair was too short to stay neat in this wind. Lizzie glanced furtively at her again. Yes, it was sticking up all over the place in gray and white tufts. Lucy's grandmothers probably had wavy white hair, neatly pinned into a respectable bun at the back. And they'd probably have been able to sit on their hair

when they were young. People did in the old days. She often read that in books.

So far Lizzie hadn't talked to any of the old ladies she had seen, and none of them had talked to her — except for a ratty one who had been looking at her own reflection in a shop window, and who had told her she was a rude little girl for staring. Lizzie, partly because she was feeling so disappointed, decided that she might as well practice on this one. She looked the right age but the wrong kind. With longer hair she'd make a good witch, though, or second cousin to a witch . . .

"I'm Lizzie Giles," Lizzie began bravely. "Who

are you?"

"Mildred Peabody, Mrs."

"Oh," said Lizzie, and stopped. What could she say about "Mildred Peabody"? She couldn't really say "that's a nice name," because she didn't think it was.

"I'm sorry," she said instead. And then wished she hadn't.

"I'm not," the woman replied pleasantly.

There was a pause.

"Where do you live? I live up there, on the seventh floor." Lizzie pointed to the nearest apartment building.

"You must get a marvelous view from your balcony. I live on Barrow Lane, in one of those little row houses near the river."

Lizzie thought how lucky Lucy was, having a grandmother who lived near the sea, but all she said was, "Sounds good. To have a whole house of your own, and go upstairs to bed like in books. We've always lived in apartments."

"Mm. I'll remember that next time my knees complain about going upstairs."

They both laughed, and Lizzie felt more comfortable. This lady wasn't as severe as she looked. After about twenty minutes of lively chatter, Lizzie decided Mildred Peabody, Mrs., wasn't exactly her idea of a grandma but she might just do.

"Do you have any children?"

"Yes, three," the old lady said rather grimly and snapped her mouth shut like a purse.

"Don't you like them?"

"I don't see much of them. Two boys and a girl. All married now."

Lizzie took a deep breath and held it. This was the important part.

"And do they have any children?"

"Yes, seven between them," Mrs. Peabody said shortly.

Lizzie could have cried. Mrs. Peabody wouldn't want any more grandchildren with seven already!

"What's the matter, child, aren't you feeling well?"

"Not very," admitted Lizzie, "now that I know you're a grandmother."

"Good gracious, what difference does that make? Don't you like grandmothers?"

"I don't know, I don't have any. My friend

Lucy goes to stay with hers."

"Does she get 'spoiled rotten'? Such an ugly phrase, but it's very expressive."

"I don't know about the rotten part, but I think so. It sounds great the way she tells it."

"Ah well, maybe hers is good at being a grandmother."

"Aren't you?" Lizzie asked, with some surprise.

"I have absolutely no idea. I've never seen any of my grandchildren. Two are in New Zealand, another pair are in Hong Kong, and three are in Canada. And I can't afford to go traipsing around the world to see them, much as I'd like to. I remember all their birthdays, of course, and send them little things for Christmas, but I have to mail them in October, so it doesn't feel the same."

Lizzie's spirits lifted. "Mrs. Peabody, would you be my grandma? By adoption?"

"Me? I'd be no good as a grandma. And I'm too old to learn . . ."

"No you're not. You could practice on me; then you'd be an expert when you see your real grandchildren."

Mrs. Peabody swiveled around on the bench and stared at Lizzie. "What an extraordinary suggestion. Do you really think I'd be okay?"

Lizzie considered carefully. "Yes," she said slowly. "I really think you'd be okay."

# Next, Convince Your Mom!

"I should really meet your mother first, Lizzie," Mrs. Peabody said. "She might not like the idea of you coming home with a new grandma. Incidentally, have you told her anything about this?"

"Not exactly," admitted Lizzie. "I'm not really allowed to talk to strangers, but you looked different. I wanted to get it right first, before I mentioned it to Mom."

Mrs. Peabody laughed. "Your mother must have a strong constitution. The introduction of a new family member surely deserves more than a 'mention,' Lizzie. It might even come as a little bit of a shock! Now, when would be a good time to visit your mother?"

"Sunday night. Mom's at work during the

week. She drives a bus all around this part of the city, up as far as the hospital, and back past my school. She's very good at it, but she gets awfully tired. Come tomorrow night and I'll tell her."

"*Ask* her, don't *tell* her," Mildred Peabody said firmly. Must have been a teacher, Lizzie thought regretfully, and she wondered what Lucy's grandma used to be.

Lizzie didn't tell her mother what the visit was all about; she just asked if a friend could come over on Sunday night.

"Not if you're going to raise the roof together, Lizzie. I'll have just gotten the place straightened up by then, and I'd like it to last."

"Oh no, Mom, she's not that way. She's a little bit older than most of my friends, and *very* sensible."

So Lizzie's mom was expecting somebody of about thirteen when she opened the door to Mrs. Peabody. And as the real reason for the visit emerged, Lizzie's mom got very quiet. Then her face began to turn red. Even her ears and the back of her neck turned red, and her eyes were stonier than Lizzie had ever seen them.

"If you'll excuse us for a moment, I'd like to have a word with my daughter," she said stiffly. "In the kitchen, Lizzie, and then . . ."

Mrs. Peabody realized immediately that Lizzie had not discussed the plan with her mother and that she herself was now in the middle of a definitely sticky situation. With a brief reproachful glance at Lizzie, who was backing away toward the kitchen, she said, "Mrs. Giles, I'm so sorry. This is obviously quite a shock. Why don't I go for a little walk and let you discuss it, and then maybe I could come back later and see how things are . . . I mean, er, well, Lizzie may have changed her mind, or . . . or something," she ended lamely.

"Why don't you do just that?" Mrs. Giles snapped nastily, opening the front door and almost pushing Mrs. Peabody out. Mrs. Peabody backed out fast, and the door banged shut in her face.

Mrs. Giles stormed into the kitchen and turned on Lizzie. "How many times have I told you never, *ever* to talk to strangers when you're by yourself? And then giving someone your address and inviting them back here! Have you gone

crazy? I must have told you a hundred times already and they tell you exactly the same at school. What about that policeman who came to your class and showed you those films? He wasn't doing it for fun, if that's what you all thought."

"Mom," wailed Lizzie, "it wasn't like that at all! She didn't talk to me first, I talked to her . . ." Her voice trailed off as she realized her mistake.

"You went up to a perfect stranger?" Mrs. Giles asked in a strangled voice. She scooped some crumbs off the table automatically and threw them into the sink. She stood with her back to Lizzie. Then she said softly, almost to herself, "If anything happened to you, I'd never forgive myself. But I can't be there all the time. Children have to learn to go out alone and take care of themselves. All I can do is warn you. Over and over again, until you can warn yourself."

Her voice faded away but she still stood there gripping the edge of the sink as if it might fall off, her head bent right down.

By this time Lizzie was crying too.

"Mom, I know what you've always told me, but it really wasn't like that."

Lizzie did her best to explain it all clearly and her mom did her best to listen very carefully, but it was difficult for both of them.

"There were lots of other people around," Lizzie ended defensively. "Anyway, I'd already worked out I could run faster than her and we weren't even sitting close together. There was miles of space between us. She couldn't even have reached me."

Mom leaned forward on her elbows and grabbed Lizzie's wrists. "All right, it wasn't quite as bad as it sounded at first. But it was a terrible risk, and I'm still shocked. It's quite hard taking care of you all by myself, and when I'm at work I just have to trust you to be sensible. We're new here, and until we make friends there's nobody else to help."

Lizzie almost said, "Well, we're not going to make many friends if we're not allowed to talk to anyone, are we?" but she swallowed the thought before it leaked out of her mouth.

"I didn't realize you wanted a grandmother so badly. It's Lucy's fault, with all her bragging. But there must be another way of doing it. We'll think of a better way together, Lizzie."

"But she was really nice," muttered Lizzie, realizing just how much she had liked Mrs. Peabody now that she was gone.

Mrs. Giles shoved a box of tissues toward Lizzie, and took a handful for herself. Still sniffling, she filled the kettle, plugged it in, and dropped a teabag into a mug. The doorbell rang. Lizzie stared at her mother.

"It's her. She's back!" she whispered.

"Heaven help us, what do we do now?" Mom breathed nervously.

Lizzie opened the door.

Mrs. Peabody smiled at her, but made no attempt to come in. She held a postcard out to Mrs. Giles, who was hovering just behind Lizzie.

"You probably want to forget the whole idea, Mrs. Giles, but I've written my name, address, and phone number here. I've lived on Barrow Lane for almost thirty years now and before I retired I was vice principal at the Girls' High School. A lot of people know me around here, so I've put some names and phone numbers on the card in case you'd like to contact them. Please do — I'm sure they wouldn't mind. And maybe we'll meet again, eh, Lizzie?" She smiled warmly and turned to go.

"I'm s-sorry," Mrs. Giles and Lizzie stammered in unison.

"No harm done. And you can't be too careful." Mrs. Peabody waved a knobby hand as she walked toward the stairwell.

Mrs. Giles shook her head violently, as if trying to rearrange her thoughts, and then called down the hall in a twisted-up voice, "Erm . . . won't you come in and have a cup of tea before you go? I was jumping to conclusions a little."

So Mrs. Peabody came back to the apartment. It felt very uncomfortable at first, but over tea and cookies she told them about herself, her family, and her little house on the river. Mrs. Giles hoped her face didn't look as blotchy as Lizzie's. Lizzie was watching her mother and thought that laughing helped. And Mrs. Peabody was certainly making them laugh about the things her friends might say about her when Mrs. Giles "checked her references."

The atmosphere improved minute by minute

and Lizzie couldn't believe that only half an hour ago her mom had been angry with her. Already they had accepted an invitation to Barrow Lane next week, and now Mrs. Peabody was saying, "I believe that in real adoptions there is a probationary period. Would it be a good idea for us to have one too? After all, I may not measure up. Lucy's grandma sounds like fierce competition and Lizzie might change her mind. I am totally inexperienced, after all."

"So is Lizzie," Mrs. Giles laughed. "She may turn out to be the kind of grandchild you would be happy to lose in the nearest fog. Have you thought of that, Liz?"

As Mrs. Peabody was getting ready to go and Mrs. Giles was helping her with her coat, she said, "Do call those phone numbers, Mrs. Giles, and don't be too hard on Lizzie. I know how worried you must have been, but I do like her enterprise. Lots of initiative."

At school the next day Lizzie said to Lucy, "Going to my grandma's on Thursday."

"Thought you didn't have one. You said you didn't."

"Well, I do. She lives on Barrow Lane."

"Oh, one of my grandmas lives in a cottage in the middle of orchards in the country, and the other one lives in a big house near the sea."

"I know all that. It's nice to have one just around the corner though. Handy for visiting."

"But I thought you said . . . Oh, there's Becky — I hope she's brought my tracksuit back," and Lucy ran off to catch Becky.

# Grandma Gets It Wrong

Mrs. Giles *did* contact the people Mrs. Peabody had suggested, just to be on the safe side.

"I spent all of my lunch hour on the phone, Lizzie. That doctor I thought would be at his clinic turned out to be a doctor of molecular biology at the university. And *he* turned out to be a she!"

Mrs. Giles was scrambling eggs in a pan while Lizzie was making some toast.

"And then I tried that minister. And he turned out to be a bishop! I almost dropped the phone. I didn't know whether to call him 'Sir' or what. It was all like that. Your Mrs. Peabody certainly has friends in high places. This is just about scrambled. Have you finished the buttering?"

"Yes, it's ready. But what did they *say* about

her?" Lizzie asked anxiously.

"Well, it was all a little embarrassing. By the time I'd explained what it was about, they started laughing. And the bishop couldn't stop. It was like a disease." She sat down, cut a square of toast, and arranged a precise square of egg on top of it. "They all seem to think she's eccentric but harmless. They hoped you'd both enjoy yourselves, and that you liked surprises, Lizzie. Why would they say a thing like that?"

"No idea. But does that mean we can have this trial — to see if it works?"

"Well, I guess so. I can't see anything wrong with an invitation to her house."

But then Mrs. Giles's work schedule was unexpectedly changed, so she had to call Mrs. Peabody to tell her that only Lizzie would be coming. Mrs. Peabody admitted that she was relieved.

"I'm in a tizzy about it already, Mrs. Giles. I don't know what the child expects, but I'll never be able to live up to it. And there aren't any evening classes to learn how to be a proper grandma! So if I have to improvise suddenly, I'd rather do it without an audience."

Mrs. Giles sympathized. "I don't really know what she expects, either. In the books she reads, grandmothers tend to be little old ladies who live in little old cottages and grow all their own vegetables. Oh, and they always have white hair in a bun and wear old-fashioned clothes and a shawl and walk with a cane. And I think they make gingerbread. Yes, and get their water from a pump in the garden."

"This is going to be terrible! I guess I could throw a bucket into the river and pretend it was a well. But nobody in their right mind would drink it!"

"Good luck." Mrs. Giles laughed and went back to work.

When Lizzie arrived at Barrow Lane, number twenty-seven looked very small. The whole row was built of dingy red bricks with purple slate roofs. Each house had one chimney and a bay window. Each house had a tiny patch of garden in front, with a path of patterned tiles leading from a curly iron gate to the front door. Every front door had a stained glass window set into the upper half. It reminded Lizzie of one of those puzzles where you have to spot the differences between almost identical pictures.

Mrs. Peabody answered the doorbell and invited her in. She looked older today than Lizzie remembered and she walked with a cane. A crocheted shawl hung unevenly from her bony shoulders and she wore a rather long skirt. Lizzie followed her through a little hallway splattered with blobs of colored light from the stained glass, and into the kitchen at the back of the house.

"Oh," Lizzie said with pleasure when she saw

the table, "it looks like a party. We only use tablecloths for parties, and that's the only time we ever make three-cornered sandwiches."

A rocking chair filled up most of the space in the little kitchen, and Mrs. Peabody lowered herself awkwardly into it. At the same moment a cat leaped across the floor with a squawk and hid under the table, watching Lizzie warily.

"You'll have to learn to keep your tail out of the way of those rockers, Pusskin. Now, where's my knitting and my specs? My legs are acting up a little today, Lizzie dear, so I didn't do any baking, I'm afraid. I had to buy a loaf instead."

"We always have this kind at home, and then it's best for toast. Grandma," she added as an afterthought. The word felt strange in her mouth.

"Come and sit here, child." Mrs. Peabody patted a small stool near her chair. Lizzie obediently sat down and for once couldn't think of anything to say. Mrs. Peabody's glasses were the half-moon kind with thin gold frames, making her look more like an ancient schoolteacher than ever. Lizzie couldn't remember her wearing them before. Maybe she

used them only for knitting, but they didn't seem to help much, because Lizzie noticed that Mrs. Peabody had dropped several stitches.

The cat returned and sat near Lizzie's feet, allowing itself to be stroked. Then it wandered away, jumped up onto the draining board, and began to lap from a small porcelain jug.

At this, Mrs. Peabody gave an undignified shriek, and managed an awkward, almost vertical takeoff from the depths of the rocking chair. The chair pivoted sideways, knocking

Lizzie off the stool. Mrs. Peabody grabbed the
table to stop herself from falling over Lizzie, but
did so nevertheless, and an avalanche of dishes
slid down the tablecloth clutched in Mrs.
Peabody's fingers. The noise was stupendous as
plates shattered and cups exploded on the floor.
Both of them were sprawled on the floor,
covered with cloth, crocheted shawl, pieces of
broken china, puddles of blackberry jam and
milk, and bent and battered sandwiches.

Lizzie felt like crying. Everything was ruined.
When she lifted a corner of the tablecloth she

thought Mrs. Peabody really *was* crying. Tears dripped down her nose, her face was all red and screwed up, and the most extraordinary noise was coming from her wide-open mouth.

Then she realized that Mrs. Peabody was positively cackling with laughter! A jam-and-crumb-covered hand patted Lizzie's knee.

"Oh, that's taught me a lesson, Lizzie. I'll never do all that again, not even for you."

The cackles continued with gasps and snorts in between, as Mrs. Peabody sat up with half a sandwich sticking to one of her shoulders and her heel in a puddle of dark lumpy jam.

"Help me up, dear, and don't look so distraught. Or are you hurt? At your age you're supposed to bounce." They both stood up and checked each other.

"No bones broken and not much blood. Except for those blackberry pools on the floor, of course. What a wreck — there's hardly anything left whole. Rescue those cupcakes, Lizzie, before you step on them. It's only the icing that's a little smooshed — they're probably still edible. Now, let's find the four corners of the tablecloth, pick up as many things as we can, and throw them into the middle of the cloth. I have to say, whenever I do something, I certainly do it thoroughly!"

She began laughing again as they dropped pieces of broken saucers, a teapot spout, and the handles of the sugar bowl on the cloth. In the end Lizzie couldn't help laughing too. Then they carried the bulging, dripping, clanking bundle straight into the garden and dropped it into a king-size trash can. Mrs. Peabody slammed the rubber lid down hard.

It took them about twenty minutes to clear up

the kitchen and another five to carry the dreadful rocking chair back to a neighbor's where it belonged. Then Mrs. Peabody made some tea and they had toast and jam and the remains of the cupcakes.

"I *am* sorry, Lizzie, but I was trying so hard to be the kind of grandma you'd read about in books. Didn't work though, did it? That awful rocking chair made me feel seasick, and I've hated that tea set for years, all those ugly pink dandelions crawling around the plates. I got the shawl and the long skirt from Goodwill and I only use that cane for blackberrying. Oh Lizzie, do you realize it's going to be very hard work for you?"

"Why, Grandma? I mean, what is?"

"You are going to have to teach me how to be a *real* grandma!"

# Manhunt

Lizzie had hidden her list inside her social studies notebook. She checked off the first entry — "1 Grandma" — with great satisfaction, then decorated the edge of the paper with a neat design of three-cornered sandwiches and iced cupcakes with cherries on top. Her new red felt-tip pen was just right for the cherries.

Mrs. Peabody began visiting the apartment quite regularly. "Could Lizzie come over after school to help me with a little ... er ... cooking?" That turned out to be brewing elderberry wine — bottles and bottles of it. Or, "If Lizzie isn't busy, would she like to play a game of cards?"

"I'm sure she'd love to." Mrs. Giles was really pleased that Lizzie and her new grandmother were getting along so well. "She's got Uno and Old Maid; she can bring them with her." But Mrs. Peabody had other ideas back at Barrow Lane.

"Let's have a game of poker. Sharpens your wits. If I teach you, you'll never be tricked in a poker game, Lizzie. Might save you a lot of trouble if you ever meet a cardsharp on a steamboat!"

It was after the poker and just before a game of gin rummy that Lizzie said, absentmindedly, "Grandma, next on my list is a grandpa. I have to start looking."

Mrs. Peabody's hands stopped in midshuffle.

"A grandpa? Of course, everybody needs a grandpa! I wish my Sam were still alive, he'd have adopted you on the spot. Pneumonia got him in the end, before he'd seen any of his grandchildren. I still miss him a lot. But now Lizzie, where will you start searching?"

"Oh, I don't really know yet. I wondered if you could help. If you're not too busy of course. It shouldn't be difficult. There are always lots of men outside the convenience store and the liquor store and there's always . . ." Her voice faded as she saw Mrs. Peabody's scandalized expression. The cold disapproving voice reminded her of her mom's the evening Lizzie had explained how she first met Mrs. Peabody.

"Lizzie, stop it! And start using your brains. Let's hear a few intelligent, *safe* suggestions!"

Lizzie gulped. Grandma sounded really fierce. She thought hard, then suggested hesitantly, "Well, what about the bowling alley? All the men look just like grandfathers there, with white mustaches. Only they're always concentrating so hard you can never talk to them. Or what about the cafeteria? Mom and I go in there sometimes, and there are always lots of old men having snacks. It looks like a senior citizens' home sometimes."

Mrs. Peabody put the cards away. "Both of those sound promising. If it's the bowling alley, I'm sure I could get us in with a team somehow. I have lots of contacts. The cafeteria idea might be quicker, though." They agreed to start there.

Lizzie and her grandma went to the cafeteria for the next three Saturday mornings, making one milk shake and one Pepsi last as long as possible. They always arrived early enough to choose an empty table for four near the window. Then Mrs. Peabody used what she called "tactics." They piled coats and empty shopping bags on the empty chairs and if a woman came toward their table looking

43

for a seat, Grandma would wave like a maniac to an imaginary friend in the line. The woman always walked past them then and found a place somewhere else. If, however, an elderly man came by, Grandma would immediately whisk the bags and coats from one of the chairs and say invitingly, "There's a spare seat here. Can I hold your tray for you while you sit down?"

It always worked. Some of the men who joined them talked too much and some were almost silent. The ones Lizzie disliked the most were the ones who brought out photographs of their grandchildren and expected her to admire them.

She soon discovered that you couldn't always judge by appearances. One elderly man looked perfect — just like a movie star grandfather — with silvery white hair and a nice tweedy suit. He pinched Lizzie's cheek playfully. It was a hard pinch and it hurt.

"I get along well with kiddies," he boasted to Mrs. Peabody, blowing pipe smoke in her face. "I'm the Santa Claus at the mall. Ho-ho-ho!" he boomed suddenly, as a demonstration. Every-

body in the cafeteria stopped talking and looked at their table. He also talked with his mouth full and soon everything was splattered with little bits of food. Lizzie hated him and decided that if he tried to pinch her cheek again, she'd bite his fingers.

Another man joined them without asking. He nibbled a chocolate cookie and didn't drop any crumbs. He talked softly and furtively; Lizzie thought he looked as if he'd escaped from prison. He asked Grandma too many questions about her house, then said urgently, "I'm looking for a room. Clean and quiet. A kindly woman like you would enjoy taking care of a lodger. Company — and a little money, no questions asked."

Lizzie felt scared, but Mrs. Peabody smiled warmly and said very sweetly, "Actually my granddaughter here spends a lot of time with me. She looks angelic now, but she's a terror in my house. The noise! And there *are* my seven other grandchildren . . ."

She winked wickedly, secretly, at Lizzie who leaned across the table and whispered loudly, "My grandma drinks. Her spare room is full of bottles!"

Both the Santa Claus man and the escaped prisoner looked shocked, and left in a hurry. Grandma and Lizzie watched them almost racing each other to the exit. It was while they were still choking with giggles that the completely wrong kind of man joined them. He was big and his huge Icelandic sweater made him look even bigger. His hair was thick and only just beginning to turn gray at the sides. The rest of it was the color of chestnuts. Lizzie watched him take off a camera and a pair of binoculars before he could drink his coffee. Grandma gave her the money to get another Pepsi, a tea, and two cinnamon buns. Lizzie stood in line thoughtfully. She hadn't decided exactly what kind of grandpa she wanted, but she was beginning to know what kind she didn't want.

# Grandma Gets It Right

When she came back with the tray, Grandma said, "Lizzie, this is Ben Bailey. He lives in one of those big old houses near the highway with his daughter and her family. And Lizzie, he's a bird-watcher too!"

Lizzie smiled politely and began to nibble her bun in rings from the outside. It just kept getting smaller and smaller until it was doll-sized. Grandma and Mr. Bailey were chatting away like old friends. He had glowing brown eyes and a charming, kindly smile, Lizzie noticed, but with five grandchildren already living in part of his house he wouldn't be interested in adopting another one. Why didn't Grandma realize this? From his outdoorsy look and smell, Lizzie guessed he'd be the kind of person who would spend hours happily lying in a ditch watching a black-throated blue warbler. She wished he would leave, so that they could concentrate on the job at hand. But he and Grandma seemed to be getting along, and he didn't leave. In fact Grandma invited him back to Barrow Lane to explore the fishing in her part of the river. And he invited her back to his house to meet his family. Several times.

Mr. Bailey now became a regular visitor at Grandma's, and Lizzie gradually stopped resenting him. But he was noisy! His explosive laugh made both Grandma and Lizzie jump, before they joined in too, and when it was too cold or wet to fish, he and Lizzie would mend things for Grandma. When Lizzie's mom saw how well he fixed things, she brought her iron and he stopped it from squirting scalding water all over everything. Then they had a dinner party to celebrate and sang silly songs until midnight.

But every time Lizzie tried to remind Grandma about the bowling alley, she just said "Soon, soon," and promptly forgot. It was a very irritating habit. And Lizzie's list was not getting any shorter.

Then one Sunday afternoon, when Mr. Bailey and Lizzie were trying to unblock a vacuum cleaner hose and Grandma was upstairs labeling her latest brew of wine, Mr. Bailey said, "I didn't know you weren't Mildred's real grandchild. I thought I'd spotted a likeness until she told me about you two adopting each other."

Lizzie stiffened, waiting for the explosive laugh. But it didn't come. Mr. Bailey extricated a wad of tissue that had been blocking the hose and held it out triumphantly for inspection. Then he said gently, "She also told me about you wanting a grandfather. If you don't have anyone else in mind, could I . . . offer my services? I know it's being a little greedy, but you don't often get the chance to choose a new grand-daughter."

"Would you, would you really?" Lizzie asked excitedly. She could hardly believe her luck.

"Why don't we try it for a little while? Like you and your grandma? The only thing is, Lizzie, I come as a package. If you adopted me, you'd be adopting my family too. That would mean a new aunt and uncle (that's my daughter Sue and her husband), and I suppose their five children would have to be, well —cousins. There are two girls older than you, a pair of

twin boys about your age, and a little girl of four. You'd better think it over, Lizzie — it's a lot to handle."

Lizzie's eyes shone but she managed to say very politely, "Oh, I think I could manage it, thank you, if *they* don't mind."

Then she raced into the hallway and yelled up the stairs, "Grandma, Grandma, you don't have to worry about the bowling alley after all. I have a new grandpa and he's just unblocked your vacuum cleaner!"

At school the next day, Lizzie and Lucy were making a Viking long-boat of papier-mâché.

"We had supper at my grandma's last night and Grandpa was there."

"But you said you didn't have a grandpa," objected Lucy, cutting out a cardboard shield.

"Well I do. He lives with my Aunt Sue and Uncle Brian. And there are five cousins. Hannah and Julia are older than us, and Jamie and Davy are identical twins as long as they keep their mouths shut, because you can only tell them apart by their teeth, and Tabitha's the youngest."

"I wish I had cousins," Lucy said enviously, "to spend vacations with. Having a lot of brothers and sisters isn't half as good, because they're always around, taking your things, and you can't ever get away from them."

"That's what I think," Lizzie said happily, though she hadn't thought of it before.

"Lizzie, I don't believe you. I think you're the biggest liar I know!"

While Mom was watching the news, Lizzie borrowed her bottle of White Out, took her felt-tip pens and schoolbag into her room, and closed the door firmly. Painting out the entries on her list for "1 brother" and "1 sister," Lizzie then blew it dry and carefully wrote "1 aunt and uncle" and underneath that, "several cousins." Then she checked off both entries very proudly, even though she knew that Grandma had actually engineered most of her new family. She drew another decorative border just inside the line of cupcakes and sandwiches — a dancing pattern of shoes, from Grandpa's fishing boots, to the little red boots of a four-year-old, to ordinary shoes and fancy shoes, with football cleats (for the twins) in between. Lizzie admired the finished pattern and wondered whether she would be a professional border decorator when she grew up. Then she heard her mother turn off the TV, so she stuck her notebook into its hiding place and went to bed.

But her list was still not quite complete. There was still "a baby." And this time she was going to do it by herself.

# The Mistake

Lizzie started looking for a baby in the park. The playground was always full of mothers with strollers or baby carriages on Saturdays. The smallest babies looked sweet, the parts you could see, but they didn't do enough to be very interesting, so Lizzie decided the bigger, sitting-up kind might be more worthwhile. She smiled at one or two, but they just looked at her like little lumps. So she tried making faces at them to get them to laugh. They certainly stopped being lumps then. One started howling and got the others going, revving up like motorcycles. Lizzie stared at them in horror and tried to tickle the nearest one's tummy to show that she was only playing.

"Get your hands off of him!"

"You leave her alone!"

"What do you think you're doing?"

Lizzie looked up to find a mob of angry mothers all shouting at her.

"I was only *looking* at them ... well, only *playing* with them ..." But nobody listened to her. Hands were unbuckling safety belts and grabbing babies, plucking children out of their nests and clutching them tightly. All she could see was wide-open mouths, howling at her. "I wasn't trying to kidnap them, if that's what you were thinking. And I don't have chicken pox or anything ..." Lizzie hurriedly backed away, and fell over someone's toy. Scrambling up, she ran. Away from the shouting mothers, away from the howling babies, all the way to the other side of the park.

She sat by the fountain to cool her face. Stupid women, she thought angrily. She was turned off of babies now. It was obviously going to be harder to find a baby than it had been to find a grandma or grandpa, because you had to get the mother's permission first. And even the most gorgeous baby might have an appalling mom. Maybe the playground was the wrong place to start.

Lizzie felt a faint pull on her sleeve, turned around, and saw a small boy wiping his face on her shirt.

"Hey you, I'm not a Kleenex!" she began angrily. Then she remembered what it felt like to be shouted at and asked more

gently, "Don't you have a tissue?"

The little boy just stared at her with his mouth open and his nose running. "Use this then," she said, fishing a clean tissue out of her pocket. He made no attempt to take it and she guessed he probably didn't know how to use it. Lizzie wiped his nose for him, not very well, since she had never wiped anyone else's nose before. His face was so grubby that pale marks showed where she had mopped up. His sweater was three sizes too big for him; the sleeves were rolled up firmly, around and around like doughnuts, and his little arms stuck through the holes.

"You are pretty disgusting," Lizzie said in a friendly voice.

The little boy looked at her, smiled, and offered her a candy. It was a piece of gum, stuck to his palm and covered with fluff.

"You keep it," she said kindly. To her horror he slapped his hand over his mouth and gobbled it up. Lizzie blinked as she thought of all the germs.

"Haven't I seen you before in the playground near the apartments? With some big kids? Red hair like yours, only darker? D'you live near here?"

The small boy began nodding his head like one of those toy dogs in the rear windows of cars. He stopped only when a commanding voice boomed across the park, "Mac, where are

you? Didn't I tell you not to wander off?"

Lizzie groaned inside. Was the whole neighborhood full of angry moms? A large woman hurried toward them, frowning fiercely and carrying a mean-looking gardening fork. She looked as if she had been made out of gray clay and dressed in yard sale clothes. Thick veins bubbled purple up her pallid bare legs.

"I been looking for you everywhere, you little stinker!"

Lizzie stood up nervously, prepared to defend the small boy. He was chewing gum noisily and didn't seem at all scared by the menacing figure.

"We were only have a little chat together," Lizzie explained nervously.

"That's a lie first of all, 'cause he don't talk," the gray face said loudly. "Can't get a word out of him, *unlike* the others, who never stop. It's all or nothing with my crew." She looked Lizzie up and down, but Lizzie couldn't decide what she was thinking.

"He shouldn't have gone off like that. He'll get himself lost one day."

"Nice little boy, isn't he?" Lizzie heard herself saying nervously. "Is his name Mike?"

"No, Mac. When he came along we'd run out of names, after all the others. *He* was a Mistake! So I asked the kids what their favorite name was and they said McDonald's. He gets called Mac for short but it's really McDonald."

Lizzie looked at Mac with renewed sympathy. His nose was running again, but she didn't dare offer him the tissue. She was a little afraid of his mom.

"I'd better be going. Bye, Mac. See you in the playground sometime."

"Thanks for watching him," Mac's mother said surprisingly.

Lizzie ran all the way home.

Her mother was putting some groceries away.

"Mom, I found this little lost boy in the park. Actually, he found me and he's named Mac. But his mother was *awful!*"

"Mac short for McDonald? I know that family. Or some of them anyway. They're the Ryans, live over on Arundel, I think. Mrs. Ryan takes my bus on Thursday afternoons and goes to their garden plot on the other side of the river. She's always got some kids with her, all redheads, and I've heard her calling the little one

'Mac.'"

"Ryans?" Lizzie remembered hearing warnings about a Ryan family at school. But nobody could be frightened of such a little boy. Maybe it was a different family, or she'd gotten the name wrong. Anyway, it was Mac she was concerned about. Mac and his alarming mother.

"She also called him a *Mistake*! I think that's awful, right in front of him. And the poor little thing was filthy, and can't talk. He should be

talking by now . . . and . . ."

Mrs. Giles suddenly looked alarmed.

"Lizzie, if you're thinking of adopting Mac, then you can forget it. Fast. The Ryans would resent it like anything. She does her best, the poor woman, taking care of eight of them, and none of them seem to go hungry. Can you imagine what it must be like to have ten people living in an apartment like this? I don't know how she manages at all. So you just steer clear, Lizzie, I mean it."

So Lizzie went to her bedroom, closed the door, and found her social studies notebook. She took out her list and felt-tip pen and drew a thick black line through "and a baby." She sat back on her heels and tried to decide whether she was a failure, or just showing common sense. Either way she still felt sad about abandoning Mac.

When she went to bed her mom came in and sat on the end.

"Lizzie, there are alternatives to adoption. Other options, I mean, like fostering and befriending. Fostering is when you take care of a child for a short time, because everyone knows the child will be going back to the real parents as soon as possible. Befriending is when you take care of somebody but they don't necessarily come to live with you. You make a special friend of them and . . . well . . . look after that person in particular.

"Why don't you become a Befriender to Mac, Lizzie? You sounded as if you liked him, in spite of his grubbiness. So why not just talk to him when you see him in the playground, or give him a push on the swings? Or just listen if he tries to talk. Tell you what, why not give him one of your old picture books — a new-looking one and write in the front, 'To Mac from Lizzie'? And put your address in it as well. Then he will know it's a present especially for him, and his mom will know where it came from, and with luck no one will be upset."

Lizzie smiled to herself in the dark. She had often thought of her mom as being a little like a beige cushion — comfortable but unexciting. Lucy's mom, who was more red-satin-with-tassels, would never have let her Lucy go near a child like Mac, in case she caught lice. Now here was her mom actually suggesting a marvelous way around the problem.

"Thanks, Mom, it's a great idea. D'you know, I bet I'm the youngest Befriender in the world. *Guinness Book of Records*, here I come!"

"Don't let it go to your head, Lizzie. And be careful, that's all."

# A Little Trouble

Lizzie chose her favorite Berenstain Bears book for Mac, wrote inside it carefully, and wrapped it in shiny green paper. She kept a lookout from her balcony high above the playground, and the next time she spotted the small figure ambling past the swings she ran down to find him. He was playing behind the benches, digging holes in the ground with a lollipop stick. A bunch of red-headed children were tormenting some boys on the swings a long way off. Those must be his brothers and sisters, Lizzie thought briefly.

"Hello, Mac. This is for you to take home and show to your mom."

He looked up at her and smiled, then took the package and began tearing off the green paper excitedly.

"D'you like the Berenstain Bears?"

Mac nodded eagerly. Then he stopped suddenly in midnod and began stuffing the half-unwrapped package inside his sweater.

"Oh, can't I read a little to you now?" Lizzie asked disappointedly as the little boy struggled to hide his book. Then she heard it, the piercing, demon shrieks and the pounding feet of his brothers and sisters.

"See you, Mac. Enjoy the book," Lizzie whispered hurriedly, edging behind the nearest bushes. She wanted to avoid any meeting with the other Ryan children because such meetings, she had noticed, usually ended in a fight. It was the thing they seemed to be best at, and because all seven of them always stuck together, they

always won. She made a point of disappearing whenever they came near. It just seemed sensible.

The next time Lizzie saw Mac he was making a road out of matchsticks and pebbles, pulling out any pieces of grass that got in the way. The rest of the Ryans were testing the destructibility of the merry-go-round, spinning it around so fast it was screaming in its cast-iron sleeve. She squatted down beside Mac.

"Like the book, Mac? Look what I found at a garage sale. It didn't cost much because it's a little scratched, but it's all there and everything works." She brought a little toy ambulance out of her pocket and put it on Mac's road.

Mac smiled happily, his eyes shining, and began making loud siren noises. "Der-der. Der-der." Lizzie showed him how to open the back doors and pull out a tiny stretcher; and she talked to him about hospitals and accidents, and dialing 911. Mac listened intently, then looked up at her and said very slowly and carefully, "Am-lance."

Lizzie hugged him with delight, and Mac laughed proudly.

"You can just cut that out. Let him go. Now!" a cold, grating voice commanded above Lizzie's head. Startled, she fell backward and sprawled on the grass. Red-haired Ryans surrounded her. Mac had vanished.

"He's not allowed to talk to strangers," the oldest girl said nastily. "Especially when they try giving him things." She tossed the little ambulance to one of her brothers.

Lizzie stood up awkwardly and tried to explain. "Mac'll tell you . . ." she began stupidly, before realizing of course that Mac couldn't tell them anything.

"We take care of him, see, and no one else lays a finger on him," the oldest girl said threateningly. Lizzie took a step backward and opened her mouth to apologize. "Who are you shoving?" another voice said spitefully, close to the back of her neck.

Hands pushed her roughly from behind. The big girl flicked her fingers at Lizzie's face, as if flicking peas off a table. It stung, and Lizzie put up her hands to protect her face. Then the others began flicking. She stumbled forward, while fingers prodded, pinched, and pulled her. Hard shoes kicked her legs and tripped her feet. She moved blindly, arms over her head to ward off the hobgoblin fingers, crouched down, hoping to push her way into a clear space. But the Ryans shoved her back, jostling her from one to the other, grabbing her shoulders and twisting her around, pulling her hair and flicking like wasp stings. She tried to shout, but each attempt was drowned by excited shrieks and screams of laughter. It was a nightmare. Lizzie realized that anybody looking would see only a mob of children laughing and dodging around. No one would guess that there was a terrified victim in the middle of the swirling huddle.

They were moving across the grass quite fast now, like some demon's dance, when the oldest girl, clearly the leader, yelled out in her scratchy, gravelly voice, "And what do we do with garbage?"

"We stuff it in the trash!" the others shrieked triumphantly, as if it was all part of a familiar game. Poor Lizzie, recoiling from the thumps and kicks and mean pinches, had no time or breath to do anything but try to keep her balance when suddenly they stopped her. She heard a heavy bolt being drawn back and the creak of a hinge. Then she was shoved violently from behind. She was in darkness. Doors clanged behind her, the bolt rattled.

As the shouts of laughter and clatter of footsteps faded into silence, Lizzie stood paralyzed with shock. She knew where she was. In one of the trash rooms. Each apartment building had one — a concrete room about the size of a garage. But many of the tenants didn't bother to use the cans, stuffing their garbage into plastic bags or cardboard boxes, which leaked and split, spilling the contents across the floor.

The stench was foul, and when at last Lizzie dared to move, the floor was slimy and her feet crunched eggshells and squashed lumps of tea bags. She sat down on top of the nearest trash can and pulled up her feet, trying to make herself as small as possible. Her eyes were getting used to the darkness now, and she could see pale pencil lines of light around the boarded-up panes in the door. Vandals had broken the glass so often that the maintenance men stopped bothering to replace it and had just nailed heavy boards over them instead. Even as she watched, the lines grew darker, as dusk deepened outside.

The silence was terrifying. Everyone else had gone home and would now be closing curtains and turning on lights and televisions. Even if Lizzie shouted, no one could hear — the ground floor of all the buildings was used only for the plumbing and heating systems. Besides, a Ryan might have been left on guard outside.

It was freezing and Lizzie pushed her hands inside her sleeves to warm them. Her mom wouldn't start worrying for ages, thinking she was probably with Lucy or Grandma, and even then she'd wait a long time before phoning, in case people thought she was fussing or over-anxious.

Lizzie strained her ears listening for rats. People had often seen rats in the trash rooms and she could feel them waiting for her in the dark. She stiffened when she heard a soft noise, a shuffling, slithery sound. She held her breath, but her heart was thumping so loudly that she couldn't really hear. Then she realized that the noise was *outside*. There were shuffling footsteps outside. Lizzie opened her mouth to shout, but only an unrecognizable quivery squeak came out, which somehow frightened her even more. Then she heard the bolt being drawn back and she toppled off the trash can, stumbling toward the door.

Strong, onion-smelling fingers caught her just before she fell, and something warm and soft wrapped itself around her legs.

"Bunions and blisters," a voice said, making the words sound like swearing. "So he *was* right all along! What are you doing in there? Some silly game, probably, but my crew is all inside with their dad, or I'd skin 'em alive. Mac kept pulling on me and pulling on me, even when I'd smacked him one, so I had to come and see what he was trying to tell me."

Lizzie discovered that it was Mac wrapped around her legs, and that it was his mother holding a weak flashlight. She began to cry with relief.

"Aren't you the girl that gave him that book? The one I seen in the park weeks ago? Nice of you. I've had to read it to him over and over again. You poor little thing, you smell horrible. You get home and into a bath, the germs in this place must be hopping. You might've been in

here all night
if it hadn't been
for Mac. He's got
brains all right,
even if he can't talk."

"Thank you, *thank you*, Mac," cried Lizzie and she hugged him tightly. Mrs. Ryan walked Lizzie to the elevator and watched her press the seventh button.

"You'll be all right now, won't you? See you." Then she hoisted Mac onto her hip, and waddled off into the darkness.

# A Little Bravery

In the elevator Lizzie looked forward to supper and sympathy. She hurt all over, and in the dim light she could see bleeding scratches and bruises on her hands and legs. She wondered what on earth Mom would say. "Told you so" probably, before putting her into a bath. As she opened the front door she heard her mother's voice, higher than usual and tight with anxiety, talking on the phone.

"But we've settled down so well here, Alan. Lizzie likes her school and has made some real friends, and I've finally gotten a really good job. It wouldn't make sense to move away now. Why Arran anyway? What's so special about Arran?"

Lizzie felt as if her legs had turned to spaghetti and leaned against the wall for support. It was

her dad. Wanting them to move again. Again! Just when she had found Lucy and Grandma and Grandpa and all the cousins. She forgot the Ryan family in this new disaster.

"Running a bed and breakfast place in the summer is all very well, but what do we do all winter?" her mother was saying worriedly.

Hot tears of anger spilled down Lizzie's face. Why was her mom so *reasonable* all the time? Why didn't she just say "No" and put the phone down? That was the only way with Dad, when he got one of his big ideas. Lizzie knew where Arran was. She had an old wooden jigsaw puzzle of the British Isles, and Arran was her favorite piece, a green island off the left-hand of Scotland, only one piece away from Glasgow.

Lizzie couldn't face going into the kitchen to hear the news of yet another move and the thought of having to pack everything all over again. She thought Mom and Dad separating had stopped all that. Were they getting back together again? Stumbling out of the apartment, she stumbled down the stairs, down, down, down, trying to run away from this new nightmare. She ran all the way to Barrow Lane and pounded on the colored glass of Grandma's front door.

Mrs. Peabody was marvelous. Recovering quickly from the shock of seeing Lizzie in such a state, she tucked her into a baggy, saggy old armchair in front of the fire and made her a cup of hot chocolate. Then she listened to a very confusing story of trash cans and islands.

"Well," she said, when Lizzie had run out of breath, "first I'm going to call your mother to let her know you're with me, before she panics. I'll ask her if you can stay for supper, then that will give us time to get you cleaned and patched up before she sees you." Mrs. Giles, struggling with the latest problem, sounded relieved to know where Lizzie was and gladly agreed to let her stay.

Then Grandma collected an assortment of Band-Aids, cotton, antiseptic, towels, and a bowl of warm water and began sponging Lizzie's cuts and bruises very gently. Questions about the injuries could wait for the moment, she decided, and thought it better to start with last things first this evening. "Wouldn't you like to go to Arran? An island might be kind of fun after all, and it's so small you'd certainly get to know people quickly."

"No, I don't want to move ever again!" Lizzie wailed. "Me and Mom are all right here and I've got you and Grandpa and Lucy and everybody! I'd like to see Dad more often, but honestly Grandma, he has itchy feet. He wouldn't last six months there and as soon as he got bored, we'd have to leave again. He actually likes moving around all the time, getting new jobs and looking for a place to live, not minding if it's horrible because then he can get busy with another move. It's exciting to begin with, but after a while you hate it. Did you know, Grandma, that this is my eleventh school? Mom and I have had enough!"

"I think he's going to be disappointed this time. I believe you have to sign a five-year lease on those apartments and I know how much your mother likes her job. She was telling me all about her 'regulars' on the bus. Your mom will dig her heels in, if I know her. So I don't think there's any real danger of another move yet Lizzie, if neither of you wants to go. No, it's the other problem that's bothering me. Those Ryan children are heading for real trouble. They're behaving like pack animals — in the worst sense of course, not like a well-disciplined team working together — more like a mob. And mobs want excitement, but don't think of consequences. What are you going to do about Mac? It's probably best to forget him, with that gang of miniterrorists on your tail."

Mrs. Peabody carefully inspected Lizzie to see if she had missed any injuries, then cleared away the towels, bowl, and cotton. "You'll survive," she said kindly, patting her gently between two bruises, on her way to the kitchen.

Lizzie had been tempted to say bravely, "I'm not afraid of *them*!" but she quickly realized that she was very much afraid, and being ambushed on the way home from school was a real possibility. Even with Lucy they would stand no chance against seven Ryans. She suddenly felt very angry at the injustice of it all.

Mrs. Peabody brought in two mugs of hot tomato soup, and the toaster, which she plugged in near Lizzie's chair.

"Grandma, it's not fair. Mac likes me and I was teaching him things. He was trying to talk to me. And his mom doesn't seem to mind. She looks funny and she shouts a lot, but I think she's friendly underneath."

Lizzie popped a slice of bread into the toaster and gazed down into it, thinking. The hot filaments looked like bright orange knitting, and the heat prickled her eyelashes. Then she faced Grandma and said fiercely, "I'm going over to see his mom. When they're *all* there. And, right in front of them, I'll ask her if I can take Mac out. For a walk or something. And if she says yes, they won't dare touch me again!"

"Sounds like stepping into a lion's den, Lizzie. Should I come with you?"

"No thanks. They might think it was because I was too scared to go by myself."

Mrs. Peabody took Lizzie home. When her mom opened the door she looked shocked at all the Band-Aids and bruises, but before she could ask what had happened, Grandma said lightly, "Had to do a little first-aid on Lizzie, I'm afraid, Mrs. Giles. Roller skates are downright dangerous, don't you think? I've told Lizzie they should be banned." She winked secretly at Lizzie, who was trying to figure out whether or not this was lying. Anyway, Mrs. Giles assumed that Lizzie had been roller-skating with Lucy, and then started talking about Dad's phone call and Arran, while Lizzie helped make coffee. Grandma was turning out to be a great partner,

a real ally.

Lizzie found the Ryans' apartment the very next Sunday. And what she had dreaded most happened. It was the stony-faced, gritty-voiced oldest girl who opened the door.

"Can I talk to your mom, please?" Lizzie asked in a clear, carrying voice. She hoped she didn't look as terrified as she felt, but she couldn't stop her heart from beating wildly. The big girl mumbled something, and was about to close the door, when Mac appeared, with a squeal of pleasure, and wedged his solid little body against it.

"Close that door, Arlene! You're letting all the heat out. Who is it anyway?"

Mrs. Ryan appeared, with a half-eaten salami sandwich in one hand. Seeing Lizzie, she flapped the sandwich at her, clearly inviting her in.

It was the messiest kitchen Lizzie had ever seen, full of people and full of things. All the people were eating. Salami sandwiches mostly, but you could see why nobody sat at the table. The table was home for a hamster cage and a tank of goldfish, a dumping ground for mending, old batteries, crumpled comic books,

and things growing in jars. Mr. Ryan was shoveling a mountain of jeans into a washing machine, holding his sandwich between his teeth when he needed both hands. He smiled at her over the heads of three of the smaller boys, who were pouring marbles down a homemade cardboard chute. It was so noisy it drowned out the TV in the corner.

When Lizzie came in, all the children fell silent, watching her warily. They even stopped chewing, though their cheeks still bulged with the last mouthful. Lizzie was aware that plenty of bruises and Band-Aids still showed. Suddenly she knew that they were all afraid *her*! Afraid that for the first time, one of their victims had come over to complain. She felt a brief flash of triumph, then remembered why she had come.

"Mr. and Mrs. Ryan, would you mind if . . . I mean . . . could I take Mac for a walk one day? Maybe just along the river to see all the boats, if he likes boats. A Saturday, I was thinking of . . . and we could take some bread for the ducks. They're very greedy, but it's really safe if you don't go too near the bank."

Mac stood beside her, patting her leg and

smiling hopefully. Clearly he understood every word. Mrs. Ryan looked at him proudly.

"That's a nice idea, Lizzie, and he loves boats, don't you, Mac? Tell you what, I'll find his old harness for you — it's safer near water and he does run off. Just until you're used to him."

Lizzie turned to Arlene, as she was the boss of the children, and said sweetly, "Are you sure you don't mind? After all, Mac is your brother. I don't have any brothers or sisters, so it would be nice to borrow one occasionally, that is, if you really don't mind."

Arlene's pale face flushed deeply.

"Oh no, we don't mind, do we? It would give us a break for once."

Lizzie didn't even bother to try the elevator. It was usually broken anyway. She bounced down all the stairs like a Ping-Pong ball, and only narrowly missed crashing into Mrs. Peabody, who just happened to be going by.

"Well, obviously all went well! I just thought I'd wander over . . ."

"In case I was murdered? Grandma, they were scared witless I was going to tell on them. I enjoyed every minute. And Mac is coming out with me next Saturday afternoon, and then one day I'm going to take him on a bus, and another time it's going to be the petting zoo, if you and Mom will come too. I've got great plans for Mac!"

And Lizzie and her grandma walked back to Barrow Lane with smiles on both their faces.

# Pom-poms and Presents

One icy morning in early December Mrs. Giles received a letter that wasn't a bill. Lizzie was trying to unstick her jacket zipper, or she would already have left for school.

"Oh my goodness! It's from Mr. Bailey's daughter. You know, your new Aunt Sue. She's invited both of us *and* Mrs. Peabody to spend Christmas with them!"

Lizzie forgot her zipper, and bounced around the kitchen squealing with joy.

"They've set up a room for me and your grandma, but would you mind having the top bunk in Tabitha's room? She's the little one, isn't she?"

"That would be great. Oh, what excellent news for a rotten old Thursday!" and Lizzie dashed off to school to tell Lucy, her open jacket flying in the freezing fog.

When she came home, however, her mother was looking worried. "We can't possibly go. Think of all the extra presents! Twenty dollars goes nowhere nowadays, and I wouldn't want to give them junk. Collecting relatives is expensive, Lizzie."

Lizzie looked downcast. Then determined.

"Mom, we'll make presents. All of them. That'll be cheaper."

"What on earth could we make? Neither of us is handy enough, and it's December already."

"I'll think of something," Lizzie promised.

"You'd better," her mom replied grimly.

At breakfast the next morning Lizzie looked smug. "Pom-pom hats!" she exploded triumphantly. "One each, in different colors, so they'll know whose is whose. In very thick yarn, so they'll be quick to knit. I can make pom-poms, I know how, and I could do the ribbing part, if you could do the casting on and decreasing part. We'd only have to get one big ball of yarn at a time, and sometimes you can get them on sale. If we started today we'd get them all

done in time."

So that was how the pom-pom hat factory
began. They knitted like crazy every evening —
soft, neutral colors for the grown-ups and bright
ones for the girls. They made identical navy ones
for the twins, but one had a red pom-pom and
one had a white one. Probably the nicest one of
all was the last one they made, a little rainbow
one from all the leftover yarn, with a jumbo
pom-pom on top, for Mac. Lizzie planned to
give it to him in the playground before the
holidays.

Lizzie and her mom were expecting to find a
fairly large Victorian house when they got off
the bus on Christmas Eve, but when they
actually stood outside Mr. Bailey's house, the
sheer size of the place made them gulp.

"It's the dark," Mom said nervously. "Things always look bigger in the dark."

"Wonder which part Grandpa lives in," Lizzie said faintly.

Her hands felt damp inside her gloves as she groped for the bell. The door itself was the size of a church door and looked as if it hadn't been opened for weeks. A disembodied voice hit them from behind, and they both jumped. "Front door's stuck. It always sticks in the winter. Come around to the back, it's what we always do."

A small figure emerged from a huge clump of rhododendrons, shook itself like a little dog, whistled piercingly into the night air, and trotted around the side of the house. An answering whistle came from somewhere in the garden.

"Davy or Jamie?" wondered Lizzie, stumbling a little as they followed the boy.

Grandpa welcomed them both at the back door and took their coats and bags.

"Mildred's arrived already. Come into the kitchen; everybody's there."

The kitchen was almost as large as the one at school, and the oven was the biggest Mrs. Giles had ever seen. Meeting the family could have been a terrible ordeal for both of them, but Aunt Sue and Uncle Brian were friendlier than they had dared to hope. At first the five children stared at Lizzie and she felt very uncomfortable, but then a pan started to boil over and Aunt Sue began yelling orders to get the table set, pronto, or nobody would be having any supper. Lizzie found herself clutching trivets and handfuls of spoons and running with the others back and forth between the kitchen and the dining room. It proved to be a terrific way to break the ice.

"Sorry Mom's so frantic," whispered Hannah,

the tallest girl. "It's our fault though. We were supposed to do this earlier," and she began feverishly counting plates.

"We were trying to wrap Grandpa's present, but it was difficult," hissed the dark-haired one, Julia, grabbing a pile of forks and dropping half of them. "Watering cans are an impossible shape to wrap."

"It's because it's Christmas Eve," whispered one of the twins, almost colliding with her.

"She'll be okay after supper, you'll see," grunted the other one, blocking a doorway with an extra chair. "Grown-ups always get high

blood pressure on Christmas Eve. It's the waiting."

"You've got the top bunk in my room," Tabitha said, so quietly that Lizzie had to bend down to ask her to say it again. "It will be nice sharing my room with you. All the others share rooms except me, and I get lonely."

It was comforting to be treated as one of the family, instead of being made to feel like a visitor, Lizzie decided, and after supper she helped make table decorations with the older girls, using tall white candles, red ornaments, and pieces of ivy. All the grown-ups were in the kitchen supposedly organizing the cooking for tomorrow, but it sounded more like a party as Mrs. Peabody was introducing them to her vintage elderberry wine. Lizzie felt proud, because she had designed the labels for that batch.

All the children were sent to bed early that evening. As Lizzie climbed quietly into the top bunk above Tabitha, who was already asleep, and saw their two stockings dangling from the ladder, she felt tingly all over from sheer happiness.

The twins woke them up at five-fifteen on Christmas Day.

"Bring your stocking and we'll go up to the girls' room and open them all together," one of the twins hissed into Lizzie's ear.

"But for goodness' sake don't drop anything, or you'll wake up Grandpa. His Christmas spirit doesn't start for another three hours or so," the other twin whispered.

"And last year he woke everybody up shouting that it was *his* house after all, and if a poor old man couldn't get any sleep on Christmas morning, he'd throw us all out into the snow."

"Only it wasn't snowing. We still had to go back to bed, though, and Grandpa said Santa Claus obviously didn't have grandchildren or he wouldn't have put cap guns in our stockings."

"Actually, I heard him say Santa Claus was a darn fool, but luckily Mom and Dad didn't hear it. He was all right by breakfast, though." They crept up the stairs, guarding their stockings with both arms, so they wouldn't bang into the banisters. "A little early, isn't it?" Julia groaned as Davy and Jamie sat down on her bed.

"We thought we'd get this part over first so you could have a really long sleep afterwards," Jamie explained cunningly.

"All right. But no harmonicas yet, and no fast-

revving cars." So they sucked on candy canes and ate chocolate ornaments, played with miniature decks of cards and metal puzzles, and had obstacle races over the comforters with joke hairy spiders. There had been one in each stocking and you could make the spiders jump by squeezing a rubber bulb at the end of a thin plastic tube. When everything had been eaten, the twins, Lizzie, and Tabitha were sent back to bed. They went quickly and without any trouble.

"Before they start complaining about all the crumbs and pieces of foil we've left in their beds." The twins giggled as they crept downstairs.

*　　*　　*

"In this family," Grandpa announced at breakfast, some time later, "everyone who isn't cooking goes to church in the morning. Hannah, Julia, and the twins are in the choir, so Lizzie, would you sit next to Tabitha and help her find the right words in her hymnal?"

"I'm allowed to sing 'la' if I don't know the words, but lots of them I do because of hearing the others practice," Tabitha said seriously. So they all trooped off to church, leaving Uncle Brian in charge of the dinner. It was all very cheerful, particularly when Jamie's joke spider fell out of his pocket as he was getting out his collection money. Mrs. Peabody picked it up and put it in her purse, and Davy giggled.

The Christmas dinner looked liked a banquet to Lizzie, and Aunt Sue said that Lizzie's table decoration had given it the finishing touch. Lizzie didn't really believe her, but it made her feel happy just the same.

Then Grandpa raised his glass: "Merry Christmas, everybody, and especially to the three new members of our family. I'd like to propose a toast to adoptions in general and to our Lizzie in particular." Everybody clapped, and Lizzie turned pink, but the twins surreptitiously pulled a cracker under the table and made everyone jump as well as laugh, so Lizzie didn't feel embarrassed for long.

It was the biggest meal she had ever eaten, and the largest dishwashing session she had ever helped with; then everybody gathered around the tree while Uncle Brian and Aunt Sue handed out presents to everyone.

Everyone except Lizzie, that is. The pom-pom hats were a great success and Grandma and Grandpa insisted on wearing theirs. Tabitha used hers to put her smallest presents in for safekeeping. Soon the floor was knee-high in wrapping paper, and everyone's arms were full of presents. Except for Lizzie's. She tried hard not to feel jealous as she saw the last tiny present being taken from beneath the tree, and just when she felt she couldn't stand it any longer, Grandpa said to the twins, "There's one left outside in the hallway. It must have been a special delivery. Bring it in, you two, but carefully, or I'll break your necks."

They staggered in carrying something large

and heavy, wrapped in a giant plastic Christmas bag. Everybody "ooh-ed" and "aah-ed" as they rushed to clear a space on the floor. Grandpa made a big fuss about not being able to find the label, and *then* not having his glasses, and *then* not being able to read the writing. The suspense was unbearable. Finally, all in a rush, he read, "It says ... 'For my special extra granddaughter, with love from us all.' Must be for you, Lizzie. You haven't gotten any presents yet. Did you think we'd forgotten you, or are you always so patient?"

"Holy cow," said Davy. "It's bigger than everyone else's put together!"

Everybody watched while Lizzie unwrapped it. Then she gasped. It was the most beautiful wooden tabletop desk, with a little brass lock and key, and her initials, *E.G.*, painted on the sloping front.

"So that's what you were making in your workshop when you wouldn't let us in!" Tabitha said accusingly.

"Oh, Grandpa," Lizzie breathed.

"Open it up," someone called out excitedly, and Lizzie unlocked the sloping lid. The inside

was full of little drawers and compartments. And inside each one was a present for her from her five new cousins, from her aunt and uncle, and from her grandma and Mom.

When she had finished unwrapping everything and thanking everybody in turn, Grandpa suggested that they have punch and Christmas cake. But he kept a restraining hand on Lizzie's shoulder. "One last thing," he said quietly, as the others trooped out. "You haven't discovered the secret place yet." He slid a small panel to one side to reveal a tiny secret space.

"I didn't want to show you in front of the others, or it wouldn't be a secret anymore. It's for special things, Lizzie." Lizzie bent her head sideways to peer in and saw an envelope. Slowly she took it out and opened it. Out fell a photograph of Mac, laughing at her from under a rainbow pom-pom hat. His nose was still running . . .

"Mildred took that the day before yesterday. She had a hard time getting a print in time. But you couldn't have one of your family missing at Christmas, could you?"

"It's perfect, Grandpa. And now we're all here! I'll never forget today, not even when I'm ancient."

"Well, let's get some punch and some cake before all the wolves finish it."

As Lizzie followed her grandpa toward the kitchen she knew what she was going to hide in the secret compartment. It had to be her list! Once she had drawn the final border decoration to finish it, of course. Lizzie smiled to herself at the thought that there would be just enough room to squeeze in a pattern of trash cans and pom-pom hats.

WANTED
1 Granny
1 Granpa
1 aunt and uncle
several cousins
and a baby